BULLIED NO MORE!

The Continuing Adventures of Emo and Chickie

Gregg F. Relyea and Joshua N. Weiss

Illustrated by Vikrant Singh (Best Studios)

About the Authors

Gregg F. Relyea, Esq.

Mr. Relyea is a lawyer, lawyer, mediator, professor, negotiation teacher and trainer. In addition to helping people resolve their disputes, he teaches negotiation and mediation at the University of San Diego, School of Law, California Western School of Law, and the University of California, San Diego (UCSD). Mr. Relyea is a member of the American Arbitration Association's Panel of Distinguished Mediators and a Practitioner/Educator member of the Association for Conflict Resolution.

Mr. Relyea co-authored "Trouble at the Watering Hole," an illustrated storybook for children ages 3 - to 12-years-old that teaches skills for resolving everyday conflicts (Resolution Press, 2018). Mr. Relyea also has authored a comprehensive text, "Negotiation, Mediation, and Dispute Resolution--Core Skills and Practices" (2018).

Joshua N. Weiss, Ph.D.

Joshua N. Weiss, Ph.D., is co-founder of the Global Negotiation Initiative at Harvard Law School and a Senior Fellow at the Harvard Negotiation Project. Dr. Weiss also is the Director of the Master's Degree in Leadership and Negotiation at Bay Bath University (Massachusetts).

Both Mr. Relyea and Dr. Weiss have authored numerous articles and publications about negotiation and mediation in professional journals, podcasts, and other publications/media.

ISBN-13: 978-0-9998344-6-6

Praise for BULLIED NO MORE!

William Ury, Co-Author of _Getting to Yes--Negotiating Agreement Without Giving In_

Conflict resolution is an essential skill for young children to learn how to resolve their problems in a constructive fashion. Gregg Relyea and Joshua Weiss' tale BULLIED NO MORE! can help children learn how to handle experiences of bullying as well as help parents engage with their children on this important issue. Highly Recommended!

Barbara Coloroso, Author of the International Bestseller, _The Bully, The Bullied, and The Not-So-Innocent Bystander_

BULLIED NO MORE! is a children's book on bullying that goes beyond and invites children to examine the roles of the bully, the bullied, and bystanders. It allows children to explore options for confronting the bullying with the intended and unintended consequences of each option. Children who are targeted can see how they can play a new role as a brave-hearted character, and how they need not do this alone. A powerfully written story that is a must read for parents, educators, and children.

ACKNOWLEDGMENTS

The authors would like to gratefully acknowledge the contributions of several people to the book. Sheila Heen, a co-author of _Difficult Conversations--How to Discuss What Matters Most_, provided valuable feedback about bullying behavior and ways to engage children in a conversation about bullying behavior.

Brian Moreland, an accomplished and award-winning author of suspense novels, including _Shadows in the Mist_, provided expert, efficient, and timely advice about moving the manuscript from paper into the digital world. Navigating the digital world simply would not have been possible without Brian's experience, expertise, and computer wizardry.

Vikrant Singh, the founder of Best Studios (division of AFI Digital Services LLP), a digital art studio, provided the colorful and energetic images in the book. His art brings the story alive and catches the eye of every child who opens the book.

Catherine Loverde provided the invaluable perspective of a Mom for this book in a way that helps reach young children in their hearts and minds.

To all the children who are bullied. You are not alone. There is help.

Be brave and talk about it with friends, family, and other people who care. And make a plan.

You have choices. Bullying can be stopped.

BULLIED NO MORE!
The Continuing Adventures of Emo and Chickie

Gregg F. Relyea and Joshua N. Weiss

Preface

BULLIED NO MORE! is a continuation of *Trouble at the Watering Hole: The Adventures of Emo and Chickie*. In this new adventure, Emo, a baby bear, and Chickie, a colorful bird who is Emo's best friend, help their friend, Bart the beaver, deal with a difficult situation related to bullying behavior.

Unfortunately, bullying has become an all too common problem in today's world. Our hope is that children who read this book, with the help of their parents or teachers, will come to understand the issue of bullying better and learn some approaches for handling it. We want children to understand they are <u>NOT ALONE</u> and should not feel as if they have to deal with these situations by themselves. Most importantly, we want children to know they have <u>CHOICES</u> if they experience bullying behavior.

This book's aim is to help parents and teachers talk about bullying behavior with their children. Too often children don't know where to turn for help, so they strike back at the person doing the bullying or they hide their feelings and don't say anything to anyone. They try to deal with bullying alone. We sincerely hope that, as children read this book together with their parents or teachers, they will come to understand options that are available to them (and perhaps even come up with their own creative options!).

Parents and teachers play a vital role in children's lives by noticing changes in their behavior. The signs are there – withdrawal and being non-communicative, prolonged periods of sadness, falling grades, defiance, and spending more time at home alone. Paying close attention to these things and talking with children when you see any of these signs can make all the difference when dealing with a difficult problem such as bullying.

Questions parents can ask their kids about bullying behavior can be found at the end of the story

Structure of the Book and How to Use It

The book examines three different ways of handling bullying behavior: fighting/hiding, talking to parents, sharing the problem with a guidance counselor.

We hope this book opens up doors to critical and creative conversations about bullying. Those conversations may very well help the children who read this story to stay safe and give them a sense of how to deal with bullying behavior should it happen to them.

Gregg F. Relyea and Joshua N. Weiss

Dark gray clouds rumbled in the distance. A late afternoon storm was rolling in. Young animals splashed and played in the watering hole. Even with the rain on its way, everyone was having a good time, except for Bart the beaver. As he did every day after school, Bart was busy helping his parents build a dam across a creek near the watering hole.

On a hot Saturday, Bart's father said to Bart, "Son, you've been working very hard lately. Why don't you take today off and have some fun?"

Bart was so excited he started doing back flips using his big flat tail to spring into the air.

Bart ran toward the watering hole as fast as his little legs would go. He picked up speed and prepared to launch himself into the cool, crisp water.He was counting down inside his head, "5, 4, 3, 2 ... "

But, before he could reach 1 and jump in, a gray furry leg came out from behind the bushes and tripped him. Bart tumbled face first into the mud, rolling forward until he came to a painful stop at the water's edge.Bart was hurt -- his face was scratched and covered in mud and his leg was bruised, but what hurt more was his pride. He felt so embarrassed.

Bart rolled on his back in pain. He closed his eyes and tried to catch his breath.

Then Bart heard something -- could it be laughter? When he opened one of his eyes, he saw a pack of young gray wolves standing around him. The biggest one, Scruffy, stood directly over Bart, grinning widely.

"What's wrong little buddy? Couldn't make it to the watering hole?"

Scruffy, who was once the smallest wolf in his family, had grown into a big, tall wolf. All the other wolves howled with laughter.

Emo and Chickie were nearby and saw what happened. Emo said, "We've seen Scruffy's older brothers and sisters picking on Scruffy. They never let him forget that he used to be the smallest."

Chickie added, "For a long time, Scruffy has been picking on other kids, and now he's doing it to little Bart."

Emo turned to Chickie, "What Scruffy is doing is so mean. The way he treats Bart and other animals is not okay. Something has to be done!"

Chickie nodded in agreement, "But what? Should we get involved? And, if so, how?"

Meanwhile, Bart picked himself up, kept his head down, and limped away. When the wolves were out of sight, he started to cry ... and continued crying all the way home.

When Bart got home, his mother asked if he had fun playing. Bart quickly rushed past her, only saying, "Yup, but I'm a little tired. I want to take a nap." His mother, busy cooking, said, "Okay, Dear," without looking up.

"Why do they have to be so mean? What did I ever do to them?" Bart thought to himself. He had no answers. He felt very sad. When his tears began to dry, his sadness turned into anger. "What right did Scruffy have to trip me? Why does everyone let him get away with this behavior? Someone should teach him a lesson!" Bart's feelings were all mixed up -- sad, mad, and frustrated. But he knew one thing for sure -- he had to get back at Scruffy and stand up for himself!

Over the next few days, Bart spied on Scruffy and his friends as they drank at the watering hole. They always came early in the morning and drank in the same spot.

Bart decided that he would get his revenge on Scruffy. He would go down to the watering hole and tie a real-looking toy alligator to a piece of string. He would put it underwater so, when Scruffy bent over to drink some water, Bart would suddenly pull up the alligator in Scruffy's face and scare him. Then Scruffy would be scared and look bad in front of his friends. Just the thought of it gave Bart a feeling of satisfaction. Bart knew it was wrong to want to hurt Scruffy. "But," Bart thought, "that's too bad, Scruffy deserves it."

The next day, Bart put his plan into action. He got up before sunrise and put the alligator underwater. Right on schedule, Scruffy and his friends walked to the watering hole. As Scruffy and his friends leaned over to drink, Bart's paw tightened on the string. He was ready to pull the alligator ... but then something made him stop. At the time, Scruffy looked so calm. He wasn't hurting anybody. He was just thirsty. Bart was also afraid of what the wolves might do if he pulled the string. Bart stopped -- he just couldn't do it.

Emo and Chickie, who were up early, saw what was happening.

Bart's plan was a total flop.

After Scruffy and his friends finished drinking, they walked away as they laughed and talked. Now, Bart felt even worse. He wasn't even brave enough to play a trick on Scruffy! He wanted to cry again. Bart knew there was more bullying behavior from Scruffy to come.

Lots of ideas came into Bart's mind. "Should I stop going to the watering hole to avoid Scruffy? Should I hide whenever I see him? Should I use the other side of the watering hole? What if I see Scruffy at school? Am I going to have to be on the lookout for him all the time? Will I always be scared of Scruffy?" All of these questions had unhappy answers.

After seeing everything happen, Emo said to Chickie, "Enough is enough. We need to find a way to help Bart."

Early the next day, Emo and Chickie found Bart rustling in the bushes, looking for twigs. Emo cleared his throat, "Umm-hmm. Good morning, Bart. We saw what happened yesterday with Scruffy. Are you okay?"

Bart jumped, "Oooh (he took a deep breath), I thought you were Scruffy. Yes, I guess I'm okay. I mean, no, I'm not okay. Ugh, I don't know! I don't understand why Scruffy and his friends pick on me. I've never done anything to them."

Emo tried to comfort him, "We know. Sometimes Scruffy does mean things. Can you think of any reason why Scruffy might be picking on you?"

Bart paused for a minute to think. "I don't know. The only thing I can think of is we have a science class together. I do well in class and Scruffy really has a hard time. I think he might feel bad about that. I wonder if that is it?"

Emo paused, "That could be."

Bart asked his friends, clenching one of his paws into a fist, "So, is there anything that I can do about this? What I'd really like to do is teach Scruffy a lesson!" He could feel the anger building up. Chickie suggested they all stop for a minute and sit down. Emo said, "Let's all take a deep breath and talk about it."

Bart felt a little better. He thought out loud, "I don't think that talking to Scruffy would help at all. He might try to make fun of me." Another idea popped into Bart's head, "I could always try to get back at Scruffy by fighting back, but Scruffy's a lot stronger and that might make things worse."

"What about talking to your parents or someone at the school about it?" Chickie asked.

"That's possible," Bart answered, "but I feel so embarrassed. I'm not sure I want to talk to anyone right now."

Emo asked Bart, "Can you think of any other ideas?"

"Well," Bart said, "Scruffy should be punished for what he's done. I could go to the guidance counselor at school if the bullying behavior continues. Even if kids call me a snitch, I don't care anymore."

Even though he wasn't sure what to do, Bart felt better just talking with Emo and Chickie. "Thanks guys," Bart said, "I really appreciate you talking with me. You gave me some good ideas."

Even though Bart, Emo, and Chickie came up with some good ideas, Bart still wasn't sure what to do. Back at home, Bart was so tired of worrying about Scruffy that he decided to close his eyes and take a nap. He hopped into bed and PLOP! Bart fell into a deep sleep.

Bart dreamed he was in science class. He was startled to hear Scruffy shout, "Hey Bart! Look at your stupid volcano! It looks like an ant hill – not a mountain! And the red paint you are using for lava looks totally fake!" Then Scruffy took his paw and knocked Bart's project to the floor ... destroying it. Other students in the class gasped and then laughed, adding to Bart's embarrassment.

15

"That's it," Bart said, "no more pushing me around." Bart jumped on Scruffy and they fell to the floor. As they were rolling around on the floor, Scruffy smeared red paint all over Bart's face. Bart did the same to Scruffy. The teacher grabbed them both and walked them to the Vice-Principal's office.

Vice-Principal Johnson was furious. There was Scruffy sitting next to little Bart -- both covered in red paint. The only thing redder was Vice-Principal Johnson's face.

In a stern voice, Vice-Principal Johnson began, "Scruffy, I've just about had enough of you! You can't seem to stay out of trouble. This is the worst thing you've done yet!"

"And you, Bart, why is a nice beaver and a good student like you getting into a fight with Scruffy?" Bart told the vice-principal about being tripped at the watering hole and the science project. Scruffy simply replied, "It was all just a joke. I didn't mean to hurt anyone. Bart needs to get a sense of humor."

Vice-Principal Johnson said, "Scruffy, that is enough! Take some responsibility for your behavior...just this once. The two of you are going to after-school detention for two full weeks."

Bart was so upset about the idea of detention that he popped awake. It had all seemed so real. But there was no red paint on him anywhere. He was at home in bed -- so he didn't really fight with Scruffy at all. Bart suddenly realized he had been dreaming.

He could see that fighting would not solve the problem and, at the same time, being scared of Scruffy all the time was no good either. Even though Bart knew it was all a bad dream, he was still upset. What was he going to do?

For a while, Bart just kept going to school every day, always looking around the corner, just in case Scruffy was there.

One day in the crowded hallway at school, Scruffy shoved Bart in his back as he was taking books out of his locker. Scruffy shouted, "Hey, Bart, Mr. Scaredy-Cat!" Startled, Bart dropped all his books and papers and pencils on the floor. All the other students laughed out loud.

Scruffy quickly walked away, not wanting to get caught. Bart, too, didn't want more trouble, so he just picked up his things as fast as he could and walked away with his head down. Bart hated being scared of Scruffy all the time, but he still didn't know what to do.

Bart decided he would just have to talk to his parents, but he was worried. Would they make things worse? What if they went to the school and got Scruffy in more trouble? Would other students make fun of Bart for getting his parents involved? Bart worried that his parents might even think everything was his fault. And, would Scruffy bully Bart more because he got in trouble? So, for a time, Bart just decided not to say anything, even though he was scared all the time. Bart felt he was all alone.

After awhile, Bart could not ignore his fears and worries any longer. Still unsure of whether it would help, one night, with Emo and Chickie by his side, Bart sat down with his parents.

"Mom, Dad, I need to talk to you about something that is hard for me to say. A kid named Scruffy has been bullying me. It has happened a few times at school, but the biggest problem was at the watering hole a few weeks ago when he tripped me."

Bart's mother jumped out of her chair and gave him a big hug. "I'm so sorry to hear that, honey. We know this is not an easy thing to talk about."

Bart's father asked, "What exactly has been happening, Bart?"

Bart continued, "Scruffy has been calling me names at school and during science class. He goes out of his way to bump into me when we pass each other in the hall. At my locker, he even pushed me so hard that I dropped all my books and papers on the floor. I try to avoid him, but it's not always possible. I worry all the time about him bothering me."

"How long has this been going on, Bart?" his mother asked.

"For a long time," Bart sighed. "But the worst thing was when Scruffy tripped me at the watering hole in front of all his friends."

Emo added, "We saw the whole thing. Scruffy did it on purpose."

For Bart, it felt good to talk about his worries. His parents listened carefully. When he was finished, they hugged him and promised they would come up with a plan very soon and talk with him about it.

After Bart fell asleep, his mother and father talked with each other. Bart's father started, "One way to handle this is to see if the problem goes away by itself. Bart mentioned that the problem at the watering hole happened a while ago and that Scruffy hasn't been as mean to him lately."

"But the bullying has been going on for a long time," Bart's mother added, "so we need to do something to protect Bart. This has gone way past the point of name-calling."

Bart's father had another idea. "We don't want this to happen again, but we also don't want to make this a big deal at school. What about contacting someone at school to let them know about the problem? And ask them to keep an eye on Scruffy?"

Bart's mother agreed, "We have to do something. Scruffy could have really hurt Bart at the watering hole and the bullying behavior at school needs to stop."

The next day Bart's parents told him about their plan to make sure he was okay with it.

"We support you and we love you, Bart," his Mom said. "We will take whatever steps are necessary to protect you." They explained they were going to contact the school and ask Vice-Principal Johnson to keep an eye on Scruffy and to check back with them in a few weeks. They told Bart to let them know if Scruffy did anything else to him and to try to ignore the small things Scruffy might do so he might lose interest in picking on Bart.

Vice-Principal Johnson kept a watchful eye on Scruffy for three weeks. Scruffy noticed that the Vice-Principal was around more than usual, so he was on his best behavior. After a few weeks, Vice-Principal contacted Bart's parents, "The bullying behavior seems to have stopped. I have told my staff about the problem and asked them to keep an eye on things. We will continue to watch Scruffy and contact you if anything happens."

Bart's parents talked with him and he confirmed that Scruffy had not been bothering him. Bart's parents also explained how Vice-Principal Johnson and the staff would be watching into the future.

At last, Bart could sleep a little better at night without worrying as much about being bullied by Scruffy. Bart knew that his parents and Vice-Principal Johnson were looking out for him, which made him feel good. Bart was glad that his parents were able to act to protect him without any other students knowing about it.

Even though the bullying had stopped for awhile, Bart still had a nagging feeling that Scruffy would do something to him. So, Bart kept a lookout for Scruffy and still tried to avoid him whenever he could. Bart still worried every day at school about Scruffy. What if Scruffy decides to pick on him again? When will it happen? Bart was looking over his shoulder all the time.

A few months later, after lunch one day, Bart saw Scruffy in the hallway. Scruffy shot Bart a dirty look, bared his teeth, and growled. Bart warned him, "Scruffy, I am telling you, if you start that again, I will get someone from the school involved."

Scruffy looked at Bart, a bit surprised, "Am I supposed to be scared? Go ahead, you little tattletale. Nobody will believe you anyway!"

After school that day, Bart went to see Mrs. Sardell, the guidance counselor. Poking his head into her office, Bart asked, "Mrs. Sardell, do you have a minute to talk?"

Looking up from her papers, Mrs. Sardell replied, "Of course, Bart. What's on your mind?"

Bart hesitated, thinking about all the problems that could come from what he was about to say, but he took a deep breath, stood up straight, and began, "I need your help. I've been bullied by another student and I want it to stop. Please, help me."

"Oh, my dear Bart, how horrible. Of course I will help," Mrs. Sardell said.

Bart shared the whole story with her, even though it was hard for him to do.

Mrs. Sardell thanked Bart for being brave and sharing what happened. She told him she would take action immediately.

After asking Bart some more questions, Mrs. Sardell talked with Emo and Chickie about what happened at the watering hole. Then, she set up a meeting with Bart and Scruffy. She wanted to talk with both of them herself.

Mrs. Sardell started, "Bart, Scruffy, I've asked you to come in today so we can talk about some things that have been happening between the two of you. Scruffy, I have been told that there have been some incidents at school and there was a problem at the watering hole between you and Bart. What happened, Scruffy?"

"Mrs. Sardell" Scruffy answered, "Nothing happened. Why would I do anything to little Bart? Who would say such a thing?"

Mrs. Sardell responded, "I had a long talk with Bart yesterday and he shared a lot of details. Some other students also saw what happened at the watering hole. Please tell me what you remember."

"Well, there's not much to say, except that I must have tripped Bart, er, um, I mean Bart must have accidentally tripped on my leg."

Mrs. Sardell asked Bart if he would like to share his story again. Bart explained what happened to him and then shared that Emo and Chickie had seen what Scruffy had done. Bart said he felt embarrassed in front of Scruffy's friends.

Mrs. Sardell asked Scruffy to repeat back what Bart said.

Scruffy slowly answered, "Hmmm, Bart said he tripped and fell."

"And what else?" Ms. Sardell asked.

"I guess he said something about me doing it on purpose," said Scruffy.

"And how did it make him feel?" Mrs. Sardell went on.

"Well, he had some bruises, so I guess it hurt," Scruffy explained.

31

"Scruffy, how would you feel if something like this happened to you?" said Mrs. Sardell.

"I wouldn't like it ... and I'd be mad," Scruffy said.

"Anything else?" Mrs. Sardell asked.

Scruffy stuttered, "Well, uh, I'm not sure. I'd probably feel bad if other people were laughing at me."

"Would you want someone to do that to you, Scruffy?" asked Mrs. Sardell.

"No, not really," Scruffy said quietly as he looked away.

Mrs. Sardell asked Bart to leave and wait in the hallway. She continued alone with Scruffy, "Are you angry at Bart for some reason?"

"No, not really," Scruffy was careful with his words.

"Until I understand what is really going on, I can't be of any help here. And I will have to tell Vice-Principal Johnson about this situation. What are you really angry about, Scruffy?" Mrs. Sardell asked gently.

"Nothing really ... well, everything. When I was little, my brothers and sisters always picked on me for being small with little patches of scruffy fur. Everyone in my family called me 'Scruffy'." He paused, then grumbled, "I really hate that name."

Scruffy continued, "And I never got help with school either. I don't really know how to study right, but I want to make the basketball team. You have to pass all your classes to be on the team. It's hard because Bart is good at science ... and all his other classes. I know it was wrong, but tripping Bart felt good at the time. It was pay-back for everything."

Mrs. Sardell was looking at Scruffy's school records when she asked him another question, "At school, everyone calls you Scruffy. What's your real name?"

"Walter," Scruffy answered, "but I'd like to go by Wally."

"Alright then, Wally, let's start by you apologizing to Bart and promising not to pick on him again." Mrs. Sardell called Bart back into her office. She explained to Bart that Scruffy wanted to be called by his real name, Wally.

Wally looked at Bart and, stumbling a little with his words, said he was sorry for bothering Bart and would not do it again. Bart felt like a ton of weight had been lifted from his shoulders, saying, "I don't want any trouble with you. And I'd be glad to call you Wally."

Mrs. Sardell said, "I think we've gone as far as we can for the day. Thank you both for your hard work. I will follow up with you in a couple weeks to see how things are going."

A few weeks passed and Bart and Wally were back in Mrs. Sardell's office. "Thank you for coming in to talk with me again. I've spoken with Wally's mother. Your family has agreed to stop calling you Scruffy." Mrs. Sardell continued, "Wally, the school will find ways to help you study for science and other classes. And I can talk with you more about ways to get along better with others, if you are willing to work with me."

"Thank you for clearing things up," Wally said, "I appreciate it."

Mrs. Sardell left them with this, "I will be available if any more problems come up. Will you boys tell me if there are any more problems?"

"Yes," Bart said. Wally nodded in agreement. "Good, then, Wally, why don't you and I meet tomorrow to talk more about schoolwork and any other issues?"

Finally, everyone understood the root of the problem. By asking the right questions, Mrs. Sardell helped everyone understand the reason Scruffy (now Wally) had been so angry and was taking it out on others.

Emo was curious, "Well, Bart, how did it go?"

"I learned some important things," Bart said. "First, I never knew that, if you get bullied, you have choices about different ways to handle it. I also found out that talking to my parents and to a guidance counselor could help a lot. I am really glad I did. It turns out that Mrs. Sardell helped everyone find out what really mattered and that made a big difference. Now I feel like things are back to normal. I can walk with my head held high and I don't have to be afraid of Wally pushing me around."

Emo smiled, but then his face turned to confusion, "Wait, who's Wally?"

Bart smiled. "That is the second thing I learned. Wally is Scruffy's real name and he hates being called Scruffy!"

Emo said, "That's interesting – I didn't know that about Wally. We're glad you worked things out together. How about going for a swim in the watering hole?"

After enjoying a playful swim in the cool water, Bart, Emo, and Chickie soaked up the sunshine. Bart could finally relax and be himself again. No more worries about Wally now that everyone understood the reason why Wally was picking on others. Bart had taken steps to protect himself by standing up to Wally and going to his parents and the school counselor. Bart's parents took action to work together with the school to make Bart safe again.

Emo asked Bart, "What if something like this happens in the future?"

Bart answered, with confidence, "Now that I know there are choices, I'm sure I can handle something like this if it ever comes up again!"

Information and Questions
Bullying Behavior

Before bullying occurs, it may be useful to have a general conversation with the children about bullying behavior.

1. **Why do you think bullying behavior happens?**

    A. Sometimes kids do things that are simply not nice, but more often there is a reason kids bully each other.

    B. Often, children bully because they have been mistreated by others or they feel they have been mistreated. As the story explains, Wally was given his nickname (Scruffy) by his family and it hurt his feelings. Scruffy's parents neglected to notice the negative impact on him of the nickname "Scruffy." When kids are mistreated, they sometimes try to handle their own pain by seeking a feeling of power or control over others. According to a survey done by Ditch the Label, a global anti-bullying organization, 1 in 3 of those who bullied said they did so because of neglect from their parents. The survey also notes that many of these kids came from bigger families where the parents don't have as much time to give attention to all the children.

    C. Bullies try to focus on something unique about children to make fun of them or to hurt them physically. Often, the qualities that a bully focuses on cannot be changed (size, strength, gender, race, physical disability, and personal appearance). These behaviors are designed to make the person doing the bullying feel superior and to make others feel inferior.

    D. According to the Ditch the Label survey, which canvassed 8,500 people about bullying, the data shows that those who bully had, themselves, experienced a stressful or traumatic situation in the past 5 years. Examples of this include parents divorcing, death of a relative or close friend, or an addition to their family that causes a lack of attention.

    E. Finally, people who have been bullied themselves are twice as likely to bully others.

2. **What is a typical reaction when bullying happens?**

    A. We all have insecurities, so we begin to believe what the person doing the bullying is saying about us is true. Are we really too short, too ugly, too fat? We criticize ourselves, instead of realizing what is happening.

    B. We often want to know why WE, in particular, are being mistreated. We ask ourselves – what did I do to deserve this (as Bart asks in the story). The reality is people who are bullied don't do anything to deserve it…they just happen to be the target of the bully's rage, frustration, and other personal problems. This is important for children to know – it is not their fault in any way.

    C. It's easy to strike back at the person doing the bullying in an effort to preserve self-esteem. Children often lash out to punish the bully and to stop the bullying behavior. Alternatively, children hide their feelings and don't talk to anyone. They turn their fear inward and might even blame themselves for being 'weak.'

3. What are some productive responses to bullying?

A. For some kids who have self-confidence, and when the bullying behavior is not serious, one response is to show the bully that their behavior does not bother them. The bully is looking to get a negative reaction.

B. It can be equally effective to do the opposite of what a bully expects (this is called "non-complementary behavior"). You will read a story below by Steven Spielberg that reinforces this point. Although it is counter-intuitive, sometimes it can actually work to 'flip the script' by using humor or, in appropriate cases, by teaming up with the bully in a way that meets the bully's own needs.

Non-Complementary Behavior This option is modeled after an example that William Ury shares in his book entitled *The Third Side* and is posted on his website. As the story goes, filmmaker Steven Spielberg had been bullied as a child. In Spielberg's words, "When I was about thirteen, one local bully gave me nothing but grief all year long. He would knock me down on the grass, or hold my head in the drinking fountain, or push my face in the dirt and give me bloody noses when we had to play football in physical education. This was somebody I feared. He was my nemesis… Then, I figured, if you can't beat him, try to get him to join you. So I said to him, 'I'm trying to make a movie about fighting the Nazis, and I want you to play the war hero.' At first, he laughed in my face, but later he said yes. He was this big fourteen-year-old who looked like John Wayne. I made him the squad leader in the film, with helmet, fatigues, and backpack. After that, he became my best friend."

C. Find someone to talk to about the issue/problem. The most important thing is not to try to deal with bullying behavior alone. If a child is not ready to talk to a parent or teacher, talking to a friend – like Bart did with Emo and Chickie -- can help.

D. Getting help from friends is important, but make sure your friends don't engage in counter bullying. As a group, tell the person using bullying behavior to stop or there will be consequences, such as telling a teacher or principal. There is power in numbers. Remind friends this is not about fighting fire with fire, but getting the bullying behavior to stop. Lashing back at someone only makes matters worse. If a child decides to fight fire with fire, the situation may very well escalate and that will be bad for everyone.

4. If kids are *engaging* in the bullying behavior, what can be done?

A. Explain to them that the bullying doesn't solve anything – highlighting all the reasons mentioned above.

B. With open communication and questions to learn more, children who bully can begin to understand *why* they are doing this to another child. If they are willing to open up about this, they are much more likely to stop. Use the example of Wally with the Guidance Counselor to help explain how to dig deeper to understand a person engaged in bullying behavior and their reasons, motivations, and perspectives.

C. Find other avenues to relieve their stress. Discovering their talents and interests and encouraging them to put their energy there can help to re-direct aggression, low self-esteem, and unresolved personal issues into a positive activity.

D. Talking to someone about their situation can really make a difference. If the child using bullying behavior will not talk to parents, there are other responsible adults who can help (including guidance counselors, private counselors, school administrators, and social workers).

E. Talking about the impact of putting someone else down to lift yourself up. Is it really an effective strategy? Or, does it add to a cycle of unhappiness, feelings of guilt and remorse, and, conversely, grandiose (but temporary) feelings of power?

F. Role reversal. Asking a child using bullying behavior to imagine what the target feels and what the target is going through can help develop empathy and a sense of compassion. Consider sharing this information: for every 10 people who are bullied, 3 of them will harm themselves as a result, 1 will go on to have a failed suicide attempt, and 1 will develop an eating disorder.

5. <u>**What is a bystander and what is their role in dealing with bullying?**</u>

A. A bystander is defined as someone who sees, hears, or otherwise witnesses a bullying incident. They either get involved (active bystander) or stay out of the situation (inactive bystander). A bystander can be a "helpful bystander," who comes to the aid of someone who is being bullied (like Emo and Chickie). A bystander also can be a "hurtful bystander," who observes bullying behavior and takes part in it or encourages it (for example, someone who joins in the bullying behavior, someone who is part of a group that is using bullying behavior, someone who records the bullying on a cell phone and shares it with others, or someone who encourages bullying behavior by cheering it on).

B. It is not uncommon for there to be bystanders when bullying occurs. It is important for kids to know that there are productive roles they can play as bystanders. These include:

    1. Simply bearing witness and noticing what is going on. Perhaps use their cellphones or other technology to capture the behavior as evidence (but not to show to other kids for entertainment value).

    2. Actively intervening on the side of the people experiencing bullying behavior. When bystanders take action it is not uncommon for bullies to back down.

    3. Serve as a sounding board or friendly ear to the person being bullied. Simply listening to that person and hearing their concerns and fears, as Chickie and Emo did with Bart, is very valuable. This helps the person being bullied to know they are not alone.

    4. Tell a parent or other adult so that they can help the person being bullied.

C. There are many examples of situations where bystanders really helped to deal with bullying behavior. It can be useful for a teacher or parent to discuss some of these with their children. There are too many examples to mention, but some can be found at:

https://www.stopbullying.gov/kids/what-you-can-do/index.html

https://www.erasebullying.ca/youth/youth-bystander.php

Questions for Kids

Fighting Back

Despite the fact that fighting or keeping quiet may feel like the only options in the moment, it will never solve the underlying issue and problem of bullying. This is a hard conversation to have with children, because cultural norms in society often tell them otherwise. In some circles, the conventional wisdom is to fight back in order to put an end to the bullying behavior. This can, at times, accomplish the desired objectives; in other cases, it can have disastrous, dangerous consequences that include escalation of the bullying behavior.

The following are questions to ask children about fighting back:

1. Did the fighting between Bart and Wally solve anything?

2. Would it solve anything for Bart to keep the bullying behavior a secret and to suffer in silence?

3. What is likely to happen in the future as a result of this incident?

4. What is the real reason Wally was bullying Bart?

5. If you think fighting is the right way to handle bullying, can you explain why and how you think it might make things better? How would it address the reasons Wally was doing this?

6. What are the risks and dangers of fighting in order to try to solve a bullying problem?

7. What are the risks and dangers of keeping quiet about bullying behavior?

Talking to Parents

When children are bullied, they may think about telling their parents, but then they often think again and decide to keep it to themselves. They start to imagine all the things kids at school will say when they find out they cannot handle their problems themselves. It is not easy for children to come to their parents and tell them about being bullied. Pride is one reason; feelings of shame can also be involved. As a parent, it is very important to be sensitive to that and to recognize how difficult it is for your child to come to you.

If a child does tell their parents they have been bullied, it is important to take action, but in a controlled manner. Of course it is upsetting, but parents need to manage their emotions in a way that shows their children that they won't make the situation worse, but they will help them through it, just like Bart's parents did.

Some questions for parents to ask:

1. Do you think it was hard for Bart to tell his parents about the situation with Scruffy? Why?

2. Have you ever had a problem like Bart's? If so, when? Why didn't you tell us/your parents?

3. Have you had a friend who had a problem like Bart's? Did they tell their parents? If not, why?

4. If you could get help from parents in a situation such as this, what would you like your parents to do? Would you like your parents to try to handle it like Bart's parents? Or some other way?

Talking to a School Guidance Counselor or Other School Official

There are many underlying causes to bullying behavior. Understanding the causes does not mean you agree with them. Bullying behavior cannot be solved unless you get to the root of the problem. In order to get to the underlying causes, it might be necessary to consult someone who is trained to ask the right questions and uncover what is REALLY going on. As we see in this ending, the guidance counselor is such a person who has that ability and their involvement can really help to mediate a problem and resolve the issue.

Some questions for children and parents to consider include:

1. Would you ever consider going to a guidance counselor or other school official to help with this kind of problem? Why? Why not?

2. When Bart and Wally sat down with the guidance counselor, she asked them lots of questions and got them to talk to each other. What did you think was a good question she asked?

3. Could you imagine sitting down with the person bullying you and talking things out? Why? Why not?

4. Were you surprised when the guidance counselor was able to get Wally to discuss what was really bothering him and why he was bullying Bart? Did that conversation make you feel bad for Wally as well? If yes, why? If no, why not?

Questions for Parents to Ask Themselves

As a parent, you play the most critical role in your child's life. The following are questions for you to consider as you think about how to help your child deal with the challenge of bullying:

1. Do you have an open channel of communication with your child? Do they come to you when they have problems? If not, what might you say to them to encourage them to do so in the future?

2. Has your child demonstrated a willingness to sit down and talk in detail with you about difficult subjects?

3. Have you actively inquired of your child, from time to time, how things are going socially at school and with their friends?

4. Have you probed beyond generalities about who their child's friends are, whether there are kids that are giving them problems, and the broader social landscape the child is dealing with every day?

5. Have you had a bullying experience as a child? As an adult? At work?

6. What method(s) did you use to handle the bullying?

7. Did your methods resolve the bullying problem? If so, how? If not, why?

8. Are you open to additional ways of handling bullying?

9. Have you taken any steps to learn about ways to handle bullying, including consulting your school, school counselor, or outside professional about any bullying of your child?

10. Have you read any books about bullying or researched the topic of bullying and ways to handle it on the Internet?

If Bullying Behavior is Aimed at Your Child

When bullying happens, both the child and parents have options. Children do not have to solve the problem of bullying behavior alone. Talking about it is a first step. Getting parents involved can help. Talking to adults with experience in handling bullying behavior, such as counselors and school officials, also can help. Asking the right questions can help. Understanding the role of bystanders, both helpful and hurtful, can help. Finally, understanding the reasons for bullying behavior can help to learn what is driving the behavior and lead to solutions that are long-lasting and positive.

A FINAL WORD --WHEN GROWN-UP KIDS ARE BULLIED

Bullying takes many forms. Your boss regularly mistreats you by being curt, engaging in daily personal attacks that shake your confidence, and withholding praise and other well-deserved recognition. Your co-workers form a group to gossip about you, to undermine your performance, and to freeze you out of opportunities for advancement. For no apparent reason, a neighbor is grumpy toward you all the time and looks for reasons to pick on you, your family--even your pets. Your own brother talks "trash" about you to other family members without any good reason.

Bullying behavior can happen to anyone at any age, at work, with peers, with colleagues, with family members, and in the community. As with children who are being bullied, you are not alone and you have choices. There are numerous resources on the Internet and elsewhere for adults who are bullied by their boss, a co-worker, a neighbor, a family member or others. The choices that are available for handling bullying behavior may be different for adults, but they still exist.

Also available through booksellers...

TROUBLE AT THE WATERING HOLE:

The Adventures of Elmo and Chickie

The forest animals have a problem—the watering hole isn't big enough. They have all the usual reasons for getting more water—who is biggest, who is strongest, and who is cleverest. But the animals are getting nowhere. Worse yet, they are fighting with each other, which won't solve anything. In *Trouble at the Watering Hole*, Emo, a baby bear cub, and his best friend, a colorful bird named "Chickie," know there must be a way to stop the fighting. Together with the forest animals, Emo and Chickie explore ways to work things out that are positive and constructive. They learn skills together and use them to work through the problem—skills that can be used to resolve everyday problems without resorting to fighting. Skills that everyone can learn.

Trouble at the Watering Hole is a breakthrough book that focuses on the skills of conflict resolution. The "how" of working things out. This fun and educational book builds a foundation for kids to learn ways to constructively resolve problems and to build strong skills that can be used to resolve conflict for the rest of their lives.

To further help teach kids conflict resolution skills, this fun and insightful children's story also contains the companion Parent/Teacher Manual.

"It would be a better world if every child had the chance to learn early in life about ways to resolve conflict through cooperation. In this wonderfully simple and instructive tale for children, accompanied by a practical teacher's guide packed with tips and exercises, Gregg Relyea and Josh Weiss make this dream possible."

—From William Ury: Co-author of *Getting to Yes* and author of *The Third Side*

CPSIA information can be obtained
at www.ICGtesting.com
Printed in the USA
FSHW011510231218
54414FS